W9-BWG-445

UH-OH,

For Linda, a dedication isn't enough, but it's a start —N.C.
For Becca, Elinor, and Simon —S.N.

A L A D D I N / An imprint of Simon & Schuster Children's Publishing Division * 1230 Avenue of the Americas, New York, NY 10020 * First Aladdin hardcover edition March 2013 * Text copyright © 2013 by Nancy Coffelt * Illustrations copyright © 2013 by Scott Nash * All rights reserved, including the right of reproduction in whole or in part in any form. * ALADDIN is a trademark of Simon & Schuster, Inc. and related logo is a registered trademark of Simon & Schuster, Inc. * For information about special discounts for bulk purchases, please contact Simon & Schuster Special Sales at 1-866-506-1949 or business@simonandschuster.com. * The Simon & Schuster Speakers Bureau can bring authors to your live event. For more information or to book an event contact the Simon & Schuster Speakers Bureau at 1-866-248-3049 or visit our website at www.simonspeakers.com. * Designed by Karin Paprocki and Scott Nash * The illustrations for this book were rendered digitally. * Manufactured in China 1212 SCP * 2 4 6 8 10 9 7 5 3 1 * Library of Congress Cataloging-in-Publication Data * Coffelt, Nancy. * Uh-oh, baby / by Nancy Coffelt ; illustrated by Scott Nash. — 1st Aladdin hardcover ed. * p. cm. * Summary: Baby Rudy tries to find a gift for his mother that she will call wonderful, but instead he hears such words as "uh-oh" as various family members encourage him to keep trying. * ISBN 978-1-4169-9149-6 (hardcover picture book) * ISBN 978-1-4424-7166-5 (eBook) * [1. Toddlers—Fiction. 2. Gifts—Fiction. 3. Family life—Fiction. 4. Humorous stories.] I. Nash, Scott, 1959- ill. II. Title. PZ7.C658Won 2012 * [E]—dc22 * 2010029299

BABY!

NANCY COFFELT

ILLUSTRATED BY
Scott Nash

ALADDIN / NEW YORK LONDON TORONTO SYDNEY NEW DELHI

Hi, Rudy! Want to play with blocks?

Hi, Rudy!
Want to help me
in the garden?

UH-OH, Rudy. We'd better go wash you off!

UNION COUNTY PUBLIC LIBRARY
316 E. Windsor St., Monroe, N.C. 28112